enchantedlionbooks.com

First published in 2015 by Enchanted Lion Books,
351 Van Brunt Street, Brooklyn, NY 11231
Copyright © 2015 by Camille Garoche
All rights reserved under International and Pan-American Copyright Conventions
A CIP record is on file with the Library of Congress
ISBN 978-1-59270-181-0
Printed in China by RR Donnelley Asia Print Solutions Ltd

10 9 8 7 6 5 4 3 2 1

First edition 2015

the Snow Rabbit

Camille Garoche

ENCHANTED LION BOOKS
NEW YORK

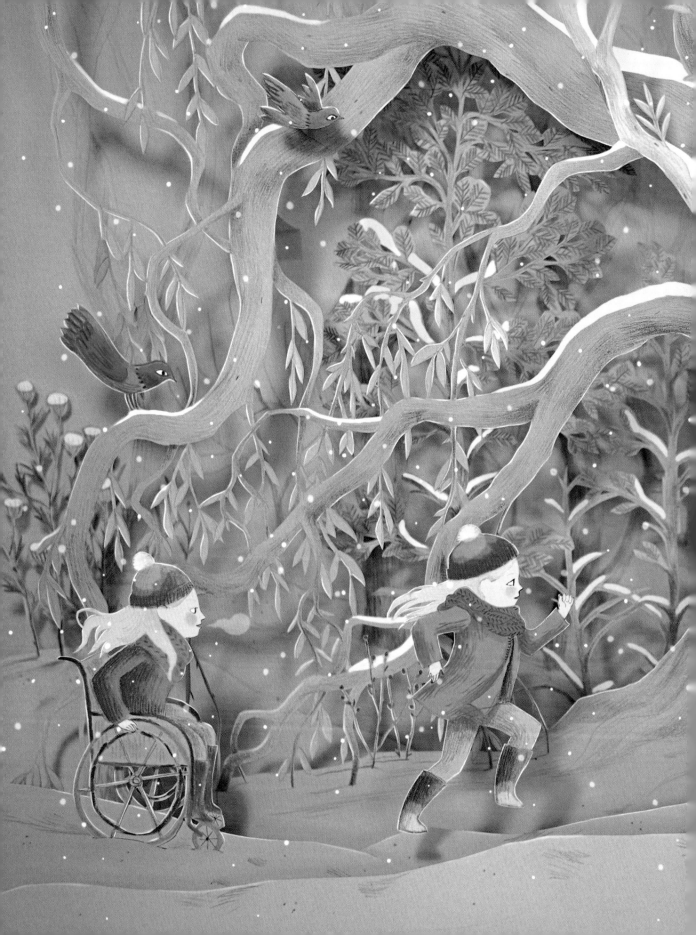

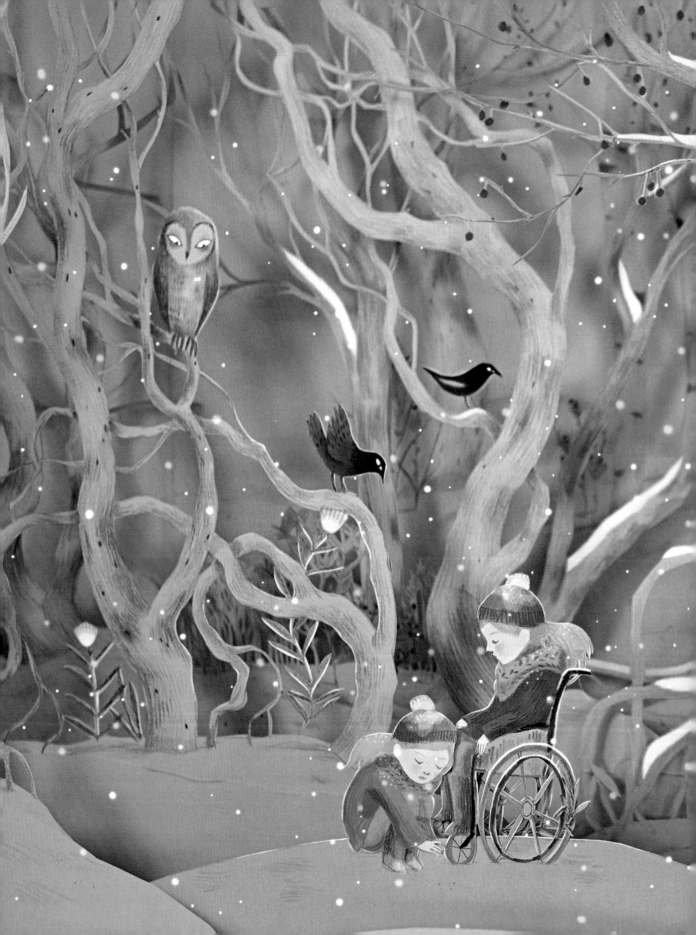